The Ocean Girl

LAVISHA

AF519894

BlueRose ONE.com
Stories Matter
NewDelhi • London

BLUEROSE PUBLISHERS
India | U.K.

BlueRose ONE
Stories Matter
NewDelhi • London

For permissions requests or inquiries regarding this publication, please contact:

BLUEROSE PUBLISHERS
www.BlueRoseONE.com
info@bluerosepublishers.com
+91 8882 898 898
+4407342408967

ISBN: 978-93-5704-033-4

Cover design: Tahira
Typesetting: Tanya Raj Upadhyay

First Edition: February 2024

PINE AVENUE

It was a normal night in California, in 2022, except for a house on the far edge of Pine Avenue. In it, there lived a small girl called Celestina. She was very smart, even though she was only in Year five, she loved reading and understanding her elder sister's high school textbook [mainly science]. Her parents were very proud of her, which made her sister, Marina, very jealous of her, so at times she hid her books, but it only made the situation worse. After they heard what Marina had done, they made her return all the books to their usual place, which was her study table. Not only that, but they also bought Celestina more books, which made Marina even more jealous. Though Celestina didn't want to make

Marina jealous, she could not help reading her textbooks, she just loved science. Celestina also possessed a great secret, though she didn't tell anyone, she was extremely scared of swimming. She had no idea why, she wasn't aquaphobic, she loved water, only that love seemed to vanish anywhere near ten feet of a swimming pool. Her sister did not know this extremely secretive secret, not till now, anyway.

One day when Celestina was going to the bus after school finished, she met Marina, so she said, "Hi Marina, you still got chocolate biscuits?"

"Is she your friend?" asked one of Marina's classmates, who did not know

Celestina. Marina then said, “No, of course not. She is so little; how can she be my friend; she is just my sister” “Well, she kind of looks as tall as you, so I got confused” Replied Marina’s friend. “ You still did not answer my question.” Celestina butted in. “No I do not, now go away.” Marina muttered, walking away with her friends. “ But where are you going, our bus is here!” Celestina exclaimed to Marina. “Oh, right.” Marina said, walking back to Celestina. “Just kidding, Sis, our bus is still, like, two to three hundred feet away.” Celestina laughed. After she stopped laughing, she asked innocently,” Want to race.” “NO!” Marina snapped. She hated it when Celestina made fun of her, especially in front of her friends. Celestina, understanding how Marina felt, said softly so that only Marina could hear, “I am sorry, sis, I won’t make fun of you again.” Marina also softened a bit and said,” It’s okay, hey, it’s quite chilly today, want to warm up” Celestina, understanding what Marina wanted to say, said, ’Okay, at the count of three, ONE TWO, and THREE.” And off they ran. They ran and ran and ran and did not stop until they reached their bus. Huffing and puffing, they climbed into the bus and sat down on their seat. Marina, with the remaining strength she had, said,” I am starving, have you got anything left to eat?” Celestina, having no strength left to talk, merrily nodded.

She opened her lunchbox and took out her last piece of chocolate biscuits, her favourite, and gave it to Marina. Marina tore it in half but Celestina gave it back to her. She said, “Don’t worry about me, I am not hungry .” ‘Are you sure you don’t want to eat this, as you just asked me in front of my friends, while also insulting and embarrassing me?” Asked Marina. ‘Yes, I am sure.” Celestina said firmly but with a small smile, Marina could be funny when she wanted to. ‘Okay, as you wish.” Answered Marina, smiling too, she loved making people laugh, it was one of her special qualities. They reached their home and got off the bus to enter the house. Both of their parents worked late since their offices were requiring, so they were used to find the house empty. For some time, they sat in silence, then Marina asked, 'Should I go and check if there is something in the pantry to eat?" Celestina nodded, saying, 'Yeah, sure, why not." Marina went to the pantry and found two candy bars there, "Hmm. Could have sworn there was only one in here yesterday." Marina wondered aloud. "But mum told you are forbidden to swear." Came Celestina's voice from the living room. Grinning to herself, Marina took the two candy bars and carried them to the living room to Celestina. She had already turned on the T.V. Marina set down the candy bars on the table and took hers. When they had finished watching and eating, they started doing their homework, that turned out so complex for both that they had only just finished when their mother came from work, which was an hour. Celestina ran to get her some water while Marina tried to helped her take out her coat, which a too complex piece of clothing for children born in 2005, so her mom ended up removing her jacket herself. “Thanks, dear.” She said, smiling. Marina, too, was grinning inwardly, her mom was being sarcastic, but not in a bad way, in fact, it was quite funny, she knew where she got her funny trait from. But her mom looked a bit ill and pale, as she had done all before six months. Celestina said, ’Mum, I think they are overworking you at the office, I have said this several times and so has Marina, why don't you leave it and try another job." Mum replied, still smiling,' It's a tempting offer, but the office I work in has a huge salary, if I work in another office, I don't quite think we will have as much luxury as we have now, in fact, I don't think we will have any luxuries at all." Celestina protested, 'But mum, who cares about money, we can be happy without it."

Celestina's mother responded gently, "Dear, that's how everybody thinks. But forget about being happy; human beings can't even live without it. Now, let's forget about my office problems. Have you finished your homework?" Her voice held a soft, concluding tone. Celestina nodded reluctantly.

They ate supper in silence, having meatloaves for dinner. That night, as Celestina settled into bed, her mother's words lingered in her mind - "human beings can't even live without it." She had always held the belief that humans were a wonderful and polite race. However, her mother's relentless work schedule troubled her. She feared that her mother's health might deteriorate if she continued to work so relentlessly.

On the lower bunk, Marina contemplated similar thoughts as Celestina, but without the pondering about humanity. She was too grown up for that, not realizing she shared these thoughts with her bunkmate.

As they were on the verge of falling asleep, a loud noise disrupted their peace. Celestina heard it clearly, while

Marina appeared undisturbed and soon drifted off. Celestina's initial thought was burglars, and she considered waking Marina. But then, she hesitated; burglars typically kept quiet. The noises downstairs weren't consistent with the stealthy actions of burglars. What if it were just two innocent cats that had slipped in through an open window? Comforted by this notion, Celestina rolled over and quickly fell back asleep.

THUD THUD THUD. Celestina awoke; it was around 1 AM. Annoyed at the 'cats' for interrupting her sleep, she was incensed, especially since she had to wake up early for the bus. She knew she wouldn't be able to fall back asleep for a while. As she got up and pushed her blankets aside, she intended to shoo the intruders away. Before she could act on that impulse, a clear voice resonated.

Celestina froze; it sounded as if someone were climbing the stairs. She had a split second to decide whether to hide. Instinctively, she knew she had to. In the nick of time, she managed to close the cupboard door behind her as she entered it. The bedroom door creaked open, and to her astonishment, two exquisite fairies floated in.

For a moment, Celestina wondered if she was still dreaming. This had to be a dream, just like the time she dreamt of a dragon lurking outside their front door, or the occasion when evil humanoid robots from Uranus had come to capture Earth. However, when one of the fairies started talking, she was taken aback.

This was peculiar; her other dreams had never involved conversations.

Curious, Celestina had to crane her neck slightly to eavesdrop on their conversation. "Poor thing, she must have hidden when she heard us coming up the stairs," one fairy said to the other, pointing towards the bedroom window. The other fairy retorted indignantly, "Oh, and do you think she would have been delighted if we had burst through her bedroom window?" They continued bickering, but Celestina had stopped paying attention; after all, they were fairies, complete with actual wings.

Celestina was overwhelmed with the feeling that she might faint or even meet her demise. "No," she sternly thought, this had to be a dream, and she needed to end it right away. Without another thought, she clenched her own arm, pinching it as hard as she could. "OUCH." Her eyes welled with tears due to the pain. She hoped that her gasp of pain had gone unnoticed by the fairies. However, her hopes were dashed when she heard a whisper, "Did you hear that?"

The sound of approaching footsteps left her feeling trapped, with no means of escape. But an unexpected savior arrived in the form of Marina. This was an unprecedented occurrence because waking up Marina from her sleep was nearly impossible, even if you clanged two plates together right next to her ear. Marina glanced at the fairies for a full second before letting out an ear-piercing scream,

"AAAAAAAAAAAAAHHHHHHHHHHH."

"Shush, please don't scream so loudly; we don't want to wake up your parents," one of the fairies implored, though it appeared that Marina relished the idea of her parents being roused from their slumber.

Just then, Celestina had had enough. She opened the cupboard door and burst out. Marina looked taken aback but remained silent. For the first time, Celestina examined the fairies. One of them had delicate purple hair and matching eyes, while the other had vibrant red hair and matching eyes. Both had fair skin and exuded a captivating beauty. The purple-haired fairy, Frista, gave off a kind vibe, whereas the red-haired fairy, Calana, appeared somewhat haughty. They were both clad in long nightdresses of a soft turquoise shade, which suited them and enhanced their beauty. They seemed no older than fifteen or sixteen.

"Who are you?" Celestina inquired, her voice surprisingly calm.

"I think you might have already guessed, but we are fairies. My name is Frista, and her name is Calana," said Frista, adding as an afterthought, "We're also twins."

"Okay, I don't mean to be rude, but that's not what I meant. What I meant was, well, I'm not quite sure how to put it, but two fairies just climbed up my stairs and called me a 'poor thing.' So, what am I supposed to make of that?" Celestina asked.

At this, the red-headed fairy, Calana, couldn't help but smirk. "You overheard that—"

"HEARD? HEARD WHAT? I SWEAR, IF YOU HARM US IN ANY WAY, I WILL RUIN YOU. UNDERSTAND? I WILL KI—" Celestina's interrupted exclamation filled the room.

But Marina could not complete her sentence, because, for the second time this night, Celestina heard footsteps climbing through the ladder, she had a split second to decide then quickly climbed into her bed. Frista and Calana also flew out of the window which Celestina could have sworn was closed a second ago. Her parents then burst into the room. They made sure everything was alright, closed the window, then left the room.

The next day passed hazily, Celestina and Marina has barely any idea of what they were doing, they got home and could not eat even anything, even though it was their favourite dish, grilled chicken. That night, instead of sleeping, Celestina and Marina waited for Frista and Calana to appear, they did not appear till midnight. When they did appear, they looked very tense, the did not say anything, the silence stretched on, until it became very uncomfortable, so Celestina mumbled on hastily and a little awkwardly, ’Um, is there anything wrong, because if there is, me and Marina would be more than happy to help you, I mean if you want us to, obviously.” If Celestina thought these words would cheer both of them up, she was clearly very wrong, both of them burst into tears, very noisy tears, which would surely carry down the stairs to their parents’ bedroom. Celestina hurried on, “Look, I don’t mean to be rude, but please don’t cry so loudly, otherwise my parents will come up.” Calana stopped crying fairly quick, while frista took a few more minutes to calm down, but when she could finally utter a few words without tears pelting from her eyes like a trapped goldfish who had just been set free, Celestina asked quickly," So what's the problem, is anything wrong? Can we help in any way?" At these words Frista started mumbling, "Oh, this is much harder than I thought, why did I sign up for this, telling you for the first time, oh, it is so hard, should have left it to the professionals- " Calana then spoke up, "Quit gibbering, let me tell you, Celestina, do not argue, do not interrupt, just listen to me, alright, this whole tale of yours starts on a cold, rainy and unfortunate night, but before I start telling you about it I just want to tell you that the people downstairs are not your parents, they just found you on the road and picked you up and decided to raise you themselves with their other girl." At this point Calana stopped talking and watched Celestina anxiously, she wanted to make sure that Celestina heard everything she said with full attention so she decided to give her a few minutes to digest this unpleasant truth before she would start talking again. Celestina looked from one guilty face to another, until she found her voice, she whispered softly to Marina, "Is it true?" Marina, her eyes sparkling with unshed tears, said," Oh, sis-" Celestina butted in, "Is it true?" Marina, her face shining with tears, whispered back, "I saw them bring you in, you were just a very small baby who looked hardly one month old." Then Marina began crying in earnest, tears spilling on to her nightdress. Celestina remained quiet, she neither cried or said anything, in fact, she thought she would never be able to do anything, and that was just the beginning bit, she thought bitterly, Calana had a lot more to say and she wondered what bad news would be worse than this, she also thought whether or not she would survive until the end of Calana's speech.

After she recovered from these uninviting thoughts, she asked Calana, “Could you please continue with the story.” Calana then replied, “Okay, if you are so sure, the second thing I would like to say to you, on a happier note, that your real parents may be alive." Celestina, when she found her voice, she said hoarsely, 'That is the happier note, they *may* be alive?" "Yep, that's right, they may be alive, and they may be anywhere in the world, good news, heh?" Calana said happily.

Celestina did not say anything, she thought if she opened her mouth she might faint before she even completed her sentence, and if she did complete her sentence, Calana would probably fly out of the window and never come back. Calana, noticing her absence of words, decided to continue the conversation anyway, so she said, "Right, the next thing I would like to tell you is-" But she never got to complete her sentence, because then Marina interrupted unexpectedly, "Please, let Celestina rest, she has heard a lot for one night, come tomorrow, then you can continue this story, just- just give her some time to digest this, please." Celestina then spoke up, "No, sis, I want to hear this tonight,

I have waited for eleven years, no more, continue, Calana." But then Frista spoke up, "I agree with Marina, Celestina simply needs time to understand this, she can't do it in one night, no kid in the whole universe can." Celestina looked furious about these people not taking her view into consideration, but before she could retort, before she could even open her mouth, Calana spoke up, "You know, I never thought I will say these words in my life, but I agree with Frista, you have heard too much for one night, we will come back tomorrow and continue this story afterwards, well then, bye."

If a longer day Celestina had than this, she certainly could not remember it, the night before had really been a lot to take in, she was trying so hard to not break into tears every second that she barely noticed that the test she had taken the day before had earned an A+. But when it was break time [Time you get to buy and eat something from the cafeteria, see, in their school you can't bring a tiffin from home to eat, it is against the school rules, so you must buy it] she could hold it no longer, she rushed to the bathroom and locked herself in one of the cubicles, and then she started crying, when she had cried to her hearts content, she stepped out of the cubicle, ah, the weight had been lifted of her shoulders, she felt full and happy again, break was almost over, but there was still time to buy and eat a chocolate croissant, or perhaps a cheese one? She had just finished nibbling the end of her croissant when the bell rang for the continuation of classes. Back came the feeling of settling gloom, mostly because of Mr. Kinto. Mr. Kinto was a very cruel teacher [Math] who thought whipping should be legal for hopeless cases, such as children. He was quite unlike his wife, Mrs. Kinto, who was also a teacher for the same school [English] and that was the class Celestina loved most because Mrs. Kinto always made classes super fun, by including games and using wacky puppet characters to make them understand something etc. And when it came to deciding which of them was better, there was no contest. So, when Celestina sat back down onto her seat, it wasn't surprising to see her not smiling, nobody smiled when it was Mr. Kinto's period, nobody felt like it since they all hated Mr. Kinto. Now, I know what you will say, hate is a strong word, but it is exactly the word you need to describe the feelings of those children. Mr. kinto even got as far as locking Jennifer Hippo

in the janitars closet for two whole whopping *hours* because she was caught trying to eat a cookie in the middle of his class.

He wouldn't even listen to her hasty explanations that as she had karate class [They had an interschool competition each year] in recess so she couldn't eat so she was very hungry. He wouldn't even try to teach them anything, he said that young children should never get the satisfaction of passing the class, that they should always stay in misery and never be happy. But little did he know that his wife, Mrs. Kinto was teaching them math if there was any extra time left in her classes, and she was such a good teacher that even on the last - minute practices the children learned the whole chapter quite easily with very little effort. So, when the children passed their math exam with flying marks, it wasn't a big surprise to Mrs. Kinto, while Mr. Kinto was simply dumbfounded.

That night, both Celestina and Marina waited painstakingly for Frista and Calana. When they did come, Celestina said straight away, "Okay, no need for all the formalities, just start and finish my story tonight and then go away, no stopping in between and no "Hi or Hello" or anything, understand?" Before Frista could respond, Calana nodded and started speaking, “Right, we stopped yesterday by telling you your parents may or may not be alive and that you are adopted, so we continue, the next thing I would like to tell you is that the house in which your parents lived was a manor, so you will have a place to live after school finished, which is an advantage, as the school and your manor are very close to each other , as I am sure you know, mermaids start their magical education when they are ready, not like other schools, which have an age limit, we told you this a bit late because we weren’t sure if you are a mermaid or not, but you are one of few who got in our school so early, others usually take a bit more time, oh, and also, you are a mermaid." Celestina then shouted at the top of her lungs, "*What?*" Calana then continued, "Yes, Yes. A mermaid, please don't interrupt so loudly, though I don't think it matters that much since I have seen for myself how deeply your parents are sleeping, and yeah, of course, your real parents also left you some inheritance, which I think will be sufficient enough until you get old enough for a job, and we also must go to the mermaid shop at Cozy Corner to get your stuff for school , oh, and if you want to you can get an animal, fish, crustacean or a baby dolphin, sorry but they are the only ones we can allow you to buy since you are young, and also, you will have to get enchanted ones since they are not allowed in the school and while you are away they need to be able to take care of themselves, well, we have to talk to your parents to explain it to them, since it will be a bit of shock for them to hear this, I think we will better handle this alone, so, bye." Celestina simply gaped at her, Calana looked at her for a second, smiling, then bolted to the door with surprising speed. By the time Celestina went to the door and whispered-screamed, "*No, don't go there*!", with a note of panic in her voice, it was too late. She could hear Calana on the stairs. Then Frista said unexpectedly, " You did better close the door, when human parents see us, they freak out, so things can get pretty nasty." Celestina did not move. "What do you mean, pretty nasty?" Frista just shook her head and told Celestina again to close the door, Celestina obeyed her this time, though rather reluctantly. When she returned, a thought struck her. "Um, Frista, I don't think I can be a mermaid, and not because I don't want to, it's because, you see, I a-am scared of w-water." Marina, who had been quiet until now, burst out, "You are *what!*" She was looking flabbergasted; she did not even look this surprised when Calana said she was a mermaid. Frista was smiling a little sadly, but when she spoke, it was with a warm voice." I know you are, but it's alright to be scared of water, most of the mermaids are before they start training, but when you finish your course of the mermaid world, I promise you will be as good as the others, oh, and Calana forgot one small detail, Marina, you are not a mermaid, but you will have superpowers, I don't know when they will show themselves, as I have never heard of such a case before, it is possibly unique, you are like and unlike Celestina. She is a mermaid, but she will be able to take a form of a mermaid , while you will not be able to, but you will have superpowers, while it is unlikely for Celestina to have any, I have never heard of such a situation, and I don't know how to break this to you, but you are also adopted, and we have no idea who your parents are, but Celestina, your parents are Olivia Kilms and David Kilms, so your name will also be Celestina Kilms, while Marina, we will just call you Marina for now." A sad kind of silence stretched across. Then Celestina, in an effort to break the nasty silence, said, "Calana is taking a lot of time, isn't she, we should really see what progress she is making." Frista and Marina nodded their agreement, and they went down the stairs. Celestina expected chaos, with things flying all over, but whatever the scenario was, it was not chaos, Calana was sitting with Celestina's stepparents, and she was being served with tea and snacks, and by the looks of it they were having a normal conversation. When Celestina's stepdad saw Marina,

Celestina and Frista approaching, he actually smiled. Yep, I am not joking, a real, warm, flattering *smile*. Celestina asked tentatively, "Um, did Calana, her name is Calana, tell you everything." Her finger had somehow found its way to Calana, though she could not remember moving it. "Yes, Yes, she told us everything, and we have never been so proud." Her stepmom smiled. Marina then said loudly, "Somebody call the ambulance, our stepparents' brains' got addled by listening to you guys." They laughed, and Marina looked even more alarmed. "No, no. We are fine." They said confidently. "Umm, are you sure?" Celestina asked timidly. They nodded, still grinning happily, as if their wish had come true. "Of course, we knew your parents, and we always thought they were hiding something, thought they were a bit mad, to be honest, but now that we think of it." At this point, Celestina's stepmom stopped speaking and burst out laughing. "But, does that mean that you will let me...will you...are you...?" Celestina couldn't stop stammering. Her parents looked at each other, the smile was now vanished, and replaced by a look of seriousness, for the first time in the night. They said, careful to keep their voice calm, "Uh, sorry dear, but we were not talking about you, we were actually talking about Marina, we think it's better if you complete your non-magical course first and then go to the mermaid world, it's for your own good you know." Celestina was flabbergasted, "But, but I, but- NO!" She screamed out the last word, she was breathing hard, she didn't know what to think, never had she a doubt, since Calana had told her there was a reserved seat for her at whatever school she was going to, that she could not come to it, and when she saw her parents smiling heartedly, her feeling had been confirmed. "Dear, I understand how you feel, but, don't you think it's better if you get a thorough understanding of our world first-" He stepmother started lovingly. "NO, I DON'T, AND WHY IN THE WORLD ARE YOU EVEN SENDING MARINA, SHE IS NOT EVEN A

MERMAID, AND, AND, WHY CAN'T I GO, ITS SO UNFAIR AND YOU DON'T EVEN CARE WHAT-." Celestina would have rumbled on further, but luckily Marina interrupted "Nor are you a mermaid." It took Celestina a few seconds to realize that she had hurt Marina's feelings. "Sorry, Marina, I didn't mean to-" "Its all right, you were angry, I get it, but I still think you should work on your anger management." Marina said. Celestina nodded, and then started speaking to her stepparents again, "Mom, Dad, I mean, stepmom, stepdad-" Then her stepmother said, in a very loud and aggressive tone, which made the hair on the back of Celestina's neck stand on end , 'Celestina our decision is final, you are not going, and nor are we buying you a baby dolphin, now go to bed, and I shall not hear a peep from you, otherwise we may cancel our idea of sending you to whatever school you are going to forever." Hot, angry, Tears filled her eyes, she stomped upstairs and covered her face with her blanket and cried silently. She must have cried for a long time, because by the time she removed her blanket, Marina was snoring, and was apparently in a deep sleep. Celestina looked at her, and hatred rose in her chest like fire in a forest, so powerful she could not control its flames, deciding it on the spot, she got up, took out her suitcase, it was pink in color and had a picture of Rose from blackpink[Her favorite band] on the front, then she packed a few clothes, some money, some eatables from the kitchen, and water, after that, with a heavy heart, she set off to face the unknown, evil world on her own. Celestina Must have walked for about a mile before the mysterious flame died, and she started missing her family terribly, she looked around, it was an unfamiliar place, and did not know the way back home, she looked around, but she could not see a single soul. There was no way she could call her parents for help, she was so scared, she began weeping uncontrollably. Then Celestina consoled herself, “Stop weeping,” she scolded herself, “You look like a small child, honestly, you make me sick." Celestina loved scolding herself, it made her think she had authority. Just when she was cheered up by this, something happened to dampen her spirits. Her eyes fell on a bright, shapeless light about 200 feet from her, it was coming closer, but that wasn't the strange thing about it, the strangest part was that every time it moved, Celestina felt a stab of pain. I wasn't normal, everyday backpain or leg pain, either. This was the real stuff, the horrible, paining for a long-time stuff. Celestina screamed and doubled over in pain. Then the bright light finally cleared and Celestina saw-well, nothing to be honest, it was empty. But Celestina did not think nobody wasn't there, because there was a certain feeling or vibe or whatever you'd call it that someone was there. Then suddenly she heard a voice say, an ice cold voice, which was a bit, well, unnerving, or something, "Ayyy, finally, finally the moment I have waited for all this time, since ten years, I finally get the chance to destroy Celestina Kilms, The Legendary Daughter Of Olivia and David kilms." Celestina's mouth was open wide, she could not understand what was happening, and could not digest it, at all. Then, suddenly, majestically, a sword appeared in front of her. The voice spoke again, "You have been given a chance to fight, Celestina, its your one last hope to live, pick up the sword, feel the warmth in your hands, and then we will battle a fair battle, in which, undoubtedly, I will win. MUHAHAHAHAHA." He gave an evil laugh at the end. And not the funny childish ones, either, this was the real, sending a shiver down your spine, laugh. Celestina, understanding the circumstances, picked up the sword, with a quivering hand. Time ticked on, every second counted, and then suddenly, without any warning, the mysterious person[Or water vapor, as I like to think of them] striked, he caught Celestina on the arm," OUCHHHHHH", arm bleeding heavily, Celestina swayed, her arm was hurting bad, she had no sense what to do, and seemed in a pretty bad position, but then, suddenly, a voice came in her head,"*You can do this!*" "What?" She whispered. Whatever the voice was, it was not her own, she thought desperately, "*Please, come back, please, tell me what I can do, oh, come on, you can't just say something inspiring and leave me to fight the battle alone, please come back, please, help me.*" But no voice answered her. Meanwhile, the mysterious person/ vapor was getting ready for another mean move, he was about to do some real damage again when this time Celestina somehow stopped his sword with her sword, with grace, as if she was born to do this. Celestina herself was surprised, she didn't know what made do it, all she knew was that when she saw him swishing down his sword her brain automatically directed her to do this. The mysterious person/vapor was also a bit taken aback, but that didn't stop him from giving another ferocious attack on that poor girl, except, Celestina was acting much more than a poor girl now, she cleverly dodged the sword, and instead took a swipe at him. But, as I said, this guy was nothing but vapor, so the sword went through him without affecting him a bit. Seeing this, he started laughing hard. But then suddenly, the sun started rising, it was sunrise. Both of the brave warriors stopped to look at this astonishing sight. Celestina heard mysterio- okay, you know, this is taking a long time to type, so I am just gonna skip ahead and type, he said, “Oh, its sunrise, gotta go, gotta go.” And then he ran off. Just then, Celestina became aware that she had lost a lot of blood, and she was becoming slightly dizzy, just before she fainted, she saw a very familiar shape running towards her, before she could make out who it was, though, she fainted.

Celestina saw something in front of her eyes, something shiny, like her sword, she tried to beat it away but when she moved her arm to hit it she saw that she was about to hit a person. “Hello Celestina.” Celestina blinked; she saw the face of a kind nurse. She looked around, it seemed she was in the hospital. The kind faced nurse called out to someone. And then many people came running in. It took Celestina some time to make them out, as all were intent upon cuddling and strangling her. They were- Her stepmother, her stepfather, Marina, Calana, Frista, and two people who looked like Calana and Frista's parents, and a few more people who she didn't know, or couldn't remember. The first person to speak to Celestina was her mom. "How stupid of you trying to run away, why didn't you just sleep, you have no idea how scared I was, that also, on your birthday!" She was half drowned in tears. Celestina thought she did better speak to her later, and turned to Frista's parents. “Hello, I am very pleased to meet you, may I ask your names?” “Of course, so stupid of us to not tell you, my name is Zack spier, and this is my wife, Nicky Spier.” The man said, He had purple eyes and red hair, while his wife had red eyes and purple hair. Now I know this is a very unusual combination, but they actually looked quite nice. They all brought snacks and juices, after asking her nurse, Celestina partied for whole whopping three hours. then, her stepparents said they wanted to tell her something. Her stepmother said, “After seeing how desperate you are to go to Martin, and seeing how you are ready to risk anything to go there, we have decided to change our decision.”

Celestina had a glass of orange juice in her hand. That came crashing down to the floor. She was speechless. Finally she said, "D-Does t-that m-m-mean –" She couldn't say more, smiling, her stepparents nodded, Celestina screamed in delight, took another glass of orange juice, and downed it in one. Then everybody began dancing happily. Everybody was happy. Except, something didn't seem nice. Marina, Frista and Calana, was looking at Celestina in a weird way. So she asked them, what's the matter, aren't you happy?" "Come out with us for a sec." Marina said, she looked nervous. "Okay." They all went outside. Then Marian started speaking, "Okay...[Really long pause]... So, this is a shock, but...............[Really long pause again].............. "Just say whatever you want too real fast." Said a really irritated Celestina who really wanted to return to the party. "As you very well know, we came through your door the first time we met you, remember? "Vividly." Celestina replied grimly. "Well. We never did tell you the actual name of the school, It is Maron, and it is named after a Merman who saved us from a terrible force, but the main point is that the person who did that terrible force is after us mermaids, and there is a high chance he will come after Maron the school, which puts you in danger." Frista concluded.

"What?"

Grinning, Celestina and Marina set down their suitcases, usual people would probably be a little less pleasant if they had to drown themselves down the Pacific Ocean to reach a school for mermaids, but not so them, they were excited to have a new day at their new school, to learn new things and make new friends. It was certainly a too exciting way to keep their school hidden, but it was worth it, the cool thing was, though, that they had been soaking wet five seconds ago, but were completely dry now. Their excitement ceased a little, when they realized they had name plates hanging from the ceiling and their own nameplates were situated at either end of the room. They had to sit separately, great. They looked at each other nodded, and set off for their own adventures independently. Under their name plates and on their tables, there was a uniform for each of them, kept neatly in a plastic bag. There were shoeboxes, inside which there were shoes and three pairs of socks. There was also a school bag, opening which they found all of their books and even some stationery!!!!They also found all of that everybody will ever need for school "Seriously, this school is dope. " Celestina jumped a foot in the air, she thought the words were in her head, but the words were coming out of someone else's mouth. Celestina looked at the girl, a pretty blonde with blue eyes who looked around eleven herself, she looked at her nameplate, there it was written *Laura Miller*. She decided to start a conversation, I mean, the sooner she had a girl gang the better, right? "Hi, I am Celestina Kilms." "I can see that." Joked the girl, pointing at the name plate above her table. Celestina smiled, her plan was going along fine, a couple more formalities and she could have a baseline for her girl gang already, a pretty girl called Laura. Who knows, they may even become best friends. A loud voice boomed in between Celestina's thoughts. "Hello new students, a warm welcome to you all." A young woman Celestina hadn't noticed before was standing at the front of the room with a mike in her hand. "I'm Amelia Williams, and I'm the Head of House for the Dolphins. Here at Maron, Dolphins is what we call the girls. You're in the girls' room right now. If any boys accidentally find their way here, please let me know immediately, and I'll direct them to the Sharks. The Sharks, by the way, are what we call the boys at Maron. Everyone clear? Great. So, find your assigned spots and remember, there's no switching places. Now, you'll notice a couple of staircases leading to the same floor, where there are many rooms. Each room has two beds, and you can choose a partner. Just keep in mind, we prefer you not pick a family member. We want everyone to focus and not stay up talking to someone they already know.

You'll be here for studying or other activities, and you'll need to attend three times a day: at eight in the morning for breakfast, at two in the afternoon for lunch, and at seven in the evening for dinner. You'll find all your school supplies on your desk, so grab them, along with your luggage. In your rooms, you'll have a designated cupboard for your belongings. Don't forget to take your locker's lock and keys from your schoolbag. Classes will run from nine in the morning until three in the afternoon.

Now, things are changing a bit. It's mandatory for all of you to stay here at the school. If you have any concerns or issues, please address them with the principal. Moving on, you'll notice a hole opening in the ceiling. Don't be alarmed. A menu will drop down, so circle your meal choices. Your selected food will be delivered through the same hole during mealtimes. Right, let's get moving."

Before Celestina could think, a hole appeared in the ceiling, and a menu was dropped onto the table in front of her. She quickly examined the options and ordered a couple of chicken drumsticks, a coke, and some vanilla ice cream. The menu was promptly retrieved, and her chosen items were delivered through the same hole.

With her food in front of her, Celestina began to ponder her situation. Families couldn't accompany students to their rooms, and the idea of rooming with Laura crossed her mind. However, she hesitated, deeming it somewhat awkward. Amelia had mentioned staying in the school building, and Celestina was relieved she had brought clothes. Her stepparents would be pleased since she had always wanted to attend a boarding school.

She couldn't contain her excitement, thinking about how cool this experience would be. She couldn't wait to share the news. Laura beat her to the question, asking, "So, want to be roommates?"

Celestina snapped out of her thoughts. Of course, she wanted to share a room; what else did she expect? "Sure," she replied.

"Cool," Laura responded enthusiastically, and Celestina considered the events of the past month. 'Cool' was the perfect word to describe this new adventure with Laura.

AUTHOR's NOTE

And here pauses this story... I hope you liked it !!, if yes, then Dear Reader, you are in luck! Because this is just the first book of a marvelous series. Want more?? then just wait and be sure to buy the next one in the series because the story will get tangled with more twists and turns!! But for now, this is.................

THE END